# This book belongs to:

..................................................

For Gabriel - F.E.

This edition first published in 2020 by Alligator Products Ltd.
Cupcake is an imprint of Alligator Products Ltd
2nd Floor, 314 Regents Park Road, London N3 2JX

www.alligatorbooks.co.uk

Written by Ruby Jones
Illustrated by Frank Endersby

Printed in China.1567

# Daisy
# Saves The Day

cupcake

Daisy was a very small dog.

Being small made her feel sad.

She couldn't run as fast as the other dogs.

She couldn't bark as loudly, or jump as high.

She wished she was bigger...

...and stronger.

When her friends went out to play, poor little Daisy had to wait at home.

"You're not big enough to play with us," they said. "You're too small and too slow!"

Daisy looked out
of the window,

as the others raced off to play in the woods.

Daisy felt lonely, she really wanted to join in.

Suddenly, Daisy heard a noise. "Help, help!"

The noise was coming from the woods.

Daisy was scared of being alone in the woods.

"Be brave, Daisy," she told herself.

Daisy followed the voice and saw that her friend Billy needed help.

"Help, I've fallen into a muddy hole," cried Billy.

"Don't worry Billy, I'll get you out," barked Daisy.

Daisy tried pulling Billy out, but she wasn't strong enough.

Daisy tried pushing Billy out, but that didn't work either.

Then Daisy had an idea. She started digging
with her paws.

Daisy's little paws
were perfect for
digging...

...and digging.

Soon Billy was free! "Thank you Daisy," he said.

"Daisy saved me!" Billy told the other dogs
what Daisy had done.

"It's not all about being big, we can all help in different ways," they all agreed.

Daisy felt so proud of herself.

"Come on Daisy," said the other dogs.
"You may be small, but you're amazing!"

The end